THE
MYSTERIOUS
OAK TREE

Written by
MARK BUCHANAN GUILLORY

Cover and Illustrations by
CRAIG HOWARTH

Published by ArkRon Limited Company

This book is based upon the author's vivid imagination.

Cover Design and Illustrations by Craig Howarth

Copy Editor: Daniel Middleton

Layout and Book Design by Daniel Middleton/Scribe Freelance

Reading Consultants: Burnadette Scott & Juliett Austin

ISBN: 978-0-9840848-0-7

Library of Congress Control Number: 2009906659

Printed in the United States of America

Dedicated to my Mom, Dad, and Brother.
Thank you for making this book possible.

—MARK

INTRODUCTION

The Mysterious Oak Tree is about two boys that go on a very exciting adventure together. Filled with plenty of laughter, tension, compassion, sadness, and joy, this story will take you on a journey to a short destination before bringing you back to reality.

The boys were playing behind a bush in the park when they realized that they were directly behind a large hill. As they traveled up the hill, they saw a huge tree at the top. By the time they made it to the tree, it was almost dark outside. As they began to go back down the hill, the tree lit up with beautiful lights that cast shadows in the dark sky. Later, the boys find out that the tree holds other mysteries about it. The excitement and mystery surrounding the tree prompted the boys to tell someone about what they had discovered. They went from place to place telling news and radio stations about what they saw, but nobody would believe them.

The Mysterious Oak Tree
By Mark Guillory

On a hot summer day, my friend Tom and I were playing behind a bush in LaQuase Park in Texas, not knowing that we were on the side of one of the biggest hills in the park. As Tom and I came from behind the bush, we were startled by the hill's enormous size! Then all of a sudden, I saw something glitter on the top of the large hill. Tom and I walked up the hill to see what was glittering and

glowing. When we reached the top of the hill, it was a big beautiful oak tree. It looked like it had more leaves than any other tree in the park.

That evening, Tom and I went back to the park to look at the tree again. We could not resist its beauty. We climbed up the tree and leaped from branch to branch, jumping off the branches to the ground. Soon, Tom and I got tired of playing and became very hungry, so we decided to eat some of the fresh oaks that grew from the oak tree. We fell asleep right by the tree.

We woke up in the night and found ourselves in the middle of the park. I looked at Tom's watch that he had purchased from the Dollar Store. It was one o'clock in the morning. To our surprise, we had slept for almost six hours. I knew my mother must have been worried sick about me.

As soon as we were about to leave, I saw the oak tree shining with many beautiful colors. I looked back, I felt as if I were in Heaven. There were red, yellow, blue, and green birds

singing on every branch of the tree. The bright colors reminded us of the first day of Spring. The tree had an appearance of a rainbow and it was full of life, with a stream of water about five feet wide running down its trunk. I thought to myself as I looked at the tree, *what a humongous tree!* I climbed to the very top of the tree, and from it, I was able to see the whole park from that spot. When I looked up, I saw a big black hole over my head. All of a sudden, it started to rain. Immediately, an area of the trunk of the tree opened as if it was welcoming us to come in from the rain. Inside the tree, we met an owl named Fester. This bird was a magical owl that depended on the tree for life. Well, from the looks of the owl, you would think that it was just an ordinary old frail bird.

Tom and I couldn't stay in the tree for long because the owl didn't want us to contaminate the tree with the foul smelling odors from our bodies. So we came down from the tree. As soon as our feet touched the ground, the glitter and glow suddenly disappeared! I looked for a second to see if it would come back on, and then we went back to my house.

We decided to gather with all of the kids at the park for a brief meeting. We asked them questions like, "Did you ever go up that hill while playing with your soccer ball?" We were trying to see if anyone had ever seen the oak tree. No one had ever seen it. We took all the kids up the hill to see the tree and the tree had mysteriously disappeared. Tom and I were stunned and paralyzed.

"I don't think anyone else has ever noticed the tree before," Tom said. "Well, I'm going to tell my mom about the exciting thing I saw last night!" he added with excitement.

"No! Don't Tom," I told him. "They will not believe you."

"So what?" said Tom.

"What do you mean?" I asked.

"I mean, what if they do believe me," Tom said.

"Well, the chances of anyone even listening to us is a million to two."

"Well, I guess we can give it a try, but I don't want to be the one on national television being criticized."

"Chill out man," I said. "We're not going to be on national television, but we are going to be on the Discovery Channel once we let reporters know about this."

"Well, let's get to it then," Tom said.

"Right!"

The next morning, no one would have known that Tom and I were both ten years of age, except for the fact that we were trembling with fear as we met with a news reporter. We could hardly get our words out as we were whispering the details of the night before to him. "All right kids, we are going to investigate around the park for any weird or suspicious events,'' said the reporter. Our hearts were racing as we returned that afternoon to see if they had unfolded this mystery. The reporter said that they saw nothing. We asked him to look again.

"That's it! You little kids are trying to fool us!'' the reporter exclaimed.

"What are you talking about?'' Tom asked. "We are telling the truth.''

"Yeah, right, like I'm suppose to believe that myth!'' the reporter shouted. "I knew something like this would happen.'' As Tom and the reporter argued,

their voices got louder and louder, and I could not even hear myself think.

After Tom and the reporter ended their argument, I decided to go to the police station to tell them everything that had happened. When we arrived inside, a man was standing asleep on the side of the wall. We walked to the back

of the station to see if anyone else was there. Another man appeared in front of me and said, "My name is Tony Jefferson. I am the Chief here. What can I do for you?"

"Excuse me," I said. "Can you help us investigate an unusual tree in the park? It's just a bit weird to us. If you could help us, we would be very thankful."

"Sure," the man said.

"The problem is that a huge oak tree has mysteriously disappeared from LaQuase Park." said Tom.

"Okay," said the man. "Now you kids should go home before your mothers become worried sick about you."

The following morning, we went to see Mr. Jefferson to see what he had learned. He informed us that there was no evidence of a huge tree being in the park. He said, "Look guys, maybe you really didn't see what you thought you saw" in a sympathetic voice.

"Yeah, he's probably right," I said, motioning to Tom. "It could just be our imagination. So I suggest that we go home. I don't want to be late for dinner tonight. Let's take the path through the park, there's something very suspicious going on with that tree." When we arrived at the park, the oak tree had re-appeared!

"The tree only appears for us!" we shouted. "How could this be? But anyway, this is fantastic!" After Tom and I had calmed down from seeing the tree again, Tom wanted to go back into the oak tree to speak with the owl. When we got inside the tree, the owl was asleep.

Tom woke him up.

"What are you doing here?" asked the owl.

"I am here to ask you a very important question," Tom said. "What time does this tree appear during the night?"

"At 9:00 p.m.," said the owl. "Once every thousand years, the tree lights up with beautiful colors celebrating its date of birth. It's my job to protect it," said the owl.

"Another thousand years! Are you serious? That's more than a lifetime," Tom said.

"It's not my fault this only occurs every one-hundred decades," the owl said.

"Well, we never expected this! I'm not giving up, this isn't over yet," said Tom.

"Are you out of your mind?" I said. "You just heard what the owl said. The tree lights up every thousand years and you are still trying to find a way to prove what we saw that night? Face it man, there is no way to prove our point, and you know that nobody will believe us without evidence."

"I can find evidence," said Tom.

"How? Nobody will even believe you, if you just come up and say, there's a magical tree inside this park, and you can't show them any evidence because it only happens once every thousand years."

"I know, but if the tree celebrates its date of birth once every thousand years, then how does the owl that lives there know that?" asked Tom.

"I should have thought of that, though it's still a good question," I said. "What if the owl is an imposter? It was big for an owl. It could be a person inside of an owl's costume."

"It just might be so," said Tom. "We'll take a look tomorrow to see if the tree appears and the owl is an imposter."

The next day, as we suspected, the tree was there. We went to see if the owl was awake, and there we saw the owl tied up in a chain on the side of the wall and another owl was in front of him.

"He must be the imposter," said Tom.

"Yeah!" I said. "It is an imposter all right, otherwise, he wouldn't have the real one tied up in a chain on the ground. Quick!

Let's listen to what they are saying."

"I tricked them into thinking that this tree lights up every thousand years," said the imposter. "Instead, it lights up once a month."

"He tricked us!" yelled Tom.

"What was that!" said the imposter. He came out to see if anyone was there.

"Quick!" I said, "Let's get out of here before he comes." So, Tom and I headed back home.

We came back to see if the imposter was still there.

"I don't see him," Tom whispered. "Let's go inside the trunk of the tree," he said.

"I don't think we should," I told him. "You saw what happened to that owl and you still want to go inside?"

"Yes," said Tom.

"Why?" I asked.

"Because, if we get the real owl out, then we can really find out what time the tree lights up."

"Didn't we hear the imposter say that the tree lights up every month."

"Yes, but what if it doesn't?" asked Tom.

Now he's just playing with me, I thought.

"Quiet, he's coming back!" said Tom.

The imposter said, "Now all I have to do is get rid of those little pests and the ancient treasure will be mine."

"What did he just say?" yelled Tom.

"What! It's those kids," said the owl.

"Oh no! We're gone, big time!" As soon as Tom opened his mouth, the imposter noticed us.

"Tom let's go before he catches one of us," I said.

"No! I'm about to show this imposter who's the boss," Tom said bravely. Then, at that moment, a man came out of the owl costume and ran toward Tom. Tom dodged him and the man tried to grab him. Tom shook him and tackled him.

"Wow! No wonder Tom's the best tackler on his football team," I said. Then I jumped in and tried to help Tom. Anyway, that's the least I could do, since Tom opened his mouth and got us into this mess. So I jumped in after Tom tackled the man to the ground and we had just enough time to unlock the real owl from the chains. Then, when Tom got the owl out of the chains, we tried to get out of there quickly, but before we could make it out, the man grabbed my leg and Tom continued to run! I fell, and the imposter tried to pull me toward him. I pushed his arm and I got back up and started to run again. Then he pulled me down again. I looked ahead of me. Tom was standing with the police and I could tell the cops couldn't believe their eyes. Then the cops came and arrested the

man. Immediately, Tom and I went to find the owl.

"Looking for me?" a voice said behind us.

"It's the owl!" Tom shouted happily.

"Because you saved me, I will grant each of you three wishes," said the owl.

"Awesome!" yelled Tom. We went to my house and suggested wishes to make. "What if we wish to have a million dollar mansion in California or our own chocolate factory?"

"Wow! That would be cool!" yelled Tom with excitement.

Well, Tom can waste his wishes on useless junk, but I'm going to wish for a mansion and a lot of money and keep investing it until it is a trillion dollars or more, I thought, after that burst of excitement from Tom.

At daybreak, I woke up in a million dollar mansion with thousands of dollars stacked up in one pile and millions of dollars in another. I went and called Tom to ask him if something had happened to him too. I started to call Tom on the phone, but I saw Tom standing in his front yard, which was across the street, staring at his home in amazement. It must have happened to him also, I thought.

"Isn't it weird how this all happened?" said Tom in a stunned voice.

"I know," I replied in a shocked tone. "It's probably because of the wish we made the other day."

"Well, if it's because of the money that we wished for, do you want to make another wish and change it all back to normal?"

"No Way!" I replied sternly. "It's good to be rich. You can buy anything you want, any food you want, any clothes you want, and any games you want."

"Sure, but what if we get everything we want and it still doesn't satisfy us?" said Tom. "Wouldn't we rather not have everything we want at one time, so we can have things to desire instead of being bored all the time?" asked Tom.

At that moment, I stopped listening to Tom. I looked back and saw the great big pool I had in the back of my mansion. I ran inside to put on some trunks to get into the pool. When I jumped into the water, it was as cold as ice in the middle of the summer. I got out quickly before I froze into an ice cube. I was shivering even more as the wind blew on my wet body. Tom came out to the pool, laughing, when he saw me shivering. We went inside so I could dry off. Later, we decided to play video games at his house. Then we had some gumbo with rice and crawfish.

I woke up the next morning and noticed that Tom's whole house was cleaned out as if he was moving. I woke Tom and asked him what was going on?

"I don't know," Tom replied in an amazed voice.

"Someone must have taken all of your stuff while we were sleeping. Maybe it was a burglar."

"Could have been," Tom replied.

"I'm going to see if my place is cleaned out also," I told Tom.

I went to my house and there was nothing in it. My place was cleaned out just as Tom's. Who could have done this? I thought.

Then I went back to Tom and asked him if I could talk to his mom about this incident. I walked up to her and asked, "Did you hear anything suspicious while you were sleeping last night?" Then all of a sudden, she started to tremble with fear; just trembling and shivering.

At that moment, Tom was coming in, and he asked his mother, "Why are you trembling?" But nothing came out of her mouth. She walked very quickly to the kitchen, moving faster and faster. "I wonder what's on her mind," Tom said quietly.

"I don't know, but it's kind of creepy," I said.

"I'm going to ask mom if we can go to the park," Tom said, while walking toward the kitchen. I walked right behind him. When we went in, we found Tom's mom on the floor having a seizure. Tom said, "Quickly! We have to call the hospital!"

I went to a phone, but I didn't know any hospital numbers.

"Get a phone book, quick!" Tom yelled.

I looked from page to page trying to find a hospital number. "I found one!" I yelled. I started dialing the numbers as fast as I could.

Finally, someone picked up. "Hello," a voice said.

"Hello ma'am. I'm calling about my friend's mom and whether you can get a doctor here right away?"

"I'll have someone there in five minutes," she said.

"Okay, thank you for all of your help." I looked back. At that moment, Tom was trying to calm his mother down. I kept looking back, trying to see if a doctor had arrived.

Then all of a sudden, a man came running in and nearly stepped on me. *I wonder if this man is a doctor or a track star,* I thought to myself. Tom on the other hand was very sad. I heard the doctor say that she was going to have to stay at the hospital for a few weeks, just enough time until they could get her heart running smoothly again. The doctor put Tom's mother in a mobile bed and pulled it out of the house and into his car.

After his mother was taken to the hospital, Tom and I played video games until midnight. For some reason, Tom started looking at the TV real hard. I observed his weird behavior for an hour. Then I walked up to him and asked what was wrong. He didn't answer. Shortly after that he walked out.

I found Tom at his breakfast table eating very slowly. "Hey, Tom!" I said. Again, he didn't answer. I started to walk to the refrigerator to get something to eat. Then words started to come out of Tom's mouth. "Have you ever had the feeling of thinking that your dear one was going to die?"

"No," I replied, "But I do know that it must feel really bad to think of it." And at that moment, the phone rang. I answered it. It was the doctor who had visited the other night.

He said, "I'm really sorry to say this, but your friend's mother has died." Then I hung up the phone. I looked back at Tom and said, "The doctor that came here last night just said that your mother has died." As soon as I said that, Tom's eyes started to get very red and watery. Then he ran into one of the rooms. I went into the room where Tom was standing. I told him that his mother was a good person and that he shouldn't worry about her because she's gone to a better place and he should be happy for her.

"You're right!" Tom yelled energetically. "I can do this. Just think positive." Tom kept saying that all day, over and over and over, until my ears almost fell off. Since he wanted to think positive, I had him to play checkers with me to take his mind off the stressful situation. As we were playing, I was learning how to play checkers better, and Tom was the perfect opponent. After playing checkers, it seemed like there was absolutely nothing else to do. So, as I sat there, a very unusual plan came to mind.

I said, "I wonder if this has something to do with the oak tree, Tom?" Then I said in a low voice, "Why don't we visit the oak tree tomorrow and ask the owl whether the three wishes he granted each of us, and the passing of your mom, had anything to do with the tree?"

"That's a good idea," said Tom.

The next day, Tom and I walked through the park and stood directly in front of the oak tree. "Mr. Owl!" yelled Tom, as we walked closer and closer to the tree. Nobody answered. As soon as we got inside the tree, Tom and I realized that it was empty. "This is weird," said Tom.

"Very!" I exclaimed. When we returned to our homes, everything was back to normal. Even Tom's mother was there.

"What an adventure!" Tom said.

"When I get older, I am sure going to enjoy telling this story to my children. I might even come up with a name to call it."

I already have a name, I said to myself, "*The Mysterious Oak Tree. Was it just a figment of our imagination?*"

ABOUT THE ILLUSTRATOR

CRAIG HOWARTH, A FREELANCE ARTIST from South Africa, has over 25 years of experience in art, illustration, and design, and has worked successfully with many authors, publishers, architects, property developers, and marketing agencies. His work is carried out swiftly and done by hand via various mediums, such as Pantone marker, ink, pencil, and oils, with some digital enhancement when required. He covers a broad spectrum of genres, including fine art, caricatures, children's book illustrations, and book covers for clients both locally and internationally.

www.ingramcontent.com/pod-product-compliance
Lightning Source LLC
Chambersburg PA
CBHW041606120626
46551CB00002B/333